nickelodeon The PENGUINS of MADAGASCAR

DREAMWORKS

Zany at the Zoo

GROSSET & DUNLAP

AN IMPRINT OF PENGUIN GROUP (USA) INC.

GROSSET & DUNLAP

Published by the Penguin Group
Penguin Group (USA) Inc., 375 Hudson Street, New York, New York 10014, USA
Penguin Group (Canada), 90 Eglinton Avenue East, Suite 700,
Toronto, Ontario M4P 2Y3, Canada
(a division of Pearson Penguin Canada Inc.)
Penguin Books Ltd., 80 Strand, London WC2R 0RL, England
Penguin Group Ireland, 25 St. Stephen's Green, Dublin 2, Ireland
(a division of Penguin Books Ltd.)
Penguin Group (Australia), 250 Camberwell Road, Camberwell,
Victoria 3124, Australia
(a division of Pearson Australia Group Pty. Ltd.)
Penguin Books India Pvt. Ltd., 11 Community Centre, Panchsheel Park,
New Delhi—110 017, India
Penguin Group (NZ), 67 Apollo Drive, Rosedale, North Shore 0632, New Zealand
(a division of Pearson New Zealand Ltd.)
Penguin Books (South Africa) (Pty.) Ltd., 24 Sturdee Avenue,
Rosebank, Johannesburg 2196, South Africa

Penguin Books Ltd., Registered Offices: 80 Strand, London WC2R 0RL, England

© 2010 Viacom International Inc. Madagascar ® DWA L.L.C. All Rights Reserved.
Published by Grosset & Dunlap, a division of Penguin Young Readers Group, 345
Hudson Street, New York, New York 10014. GROSSET & DUNLAP is a trademark
of Penguin Group (USA) Inc. Printed in the U.S.A.

Library of Congress Control Number: 2009029466

ISBN 978-0-448-45258-6   10 9 8 7 6 5 4 3 2 1

nickelodeon The PENGUINS of MADAGASCAR

DREAMWORKS

ZANY AT THE ZOO

BY DAVID ROSENBERG

Grosset & Dunlap

AN IMPRINT OF PENGUIN GROUP (USA) INC.

It's a Penguin Party!

Q: What's black-and-white and black-and-white and makes you dance?

A: A penguin playing the piano

Q: What's black-and-white and floats through the air?

A: A penguin skydiving

Q: What's black-and-white and red all over?

A: A penguin with a sunburn

Q: What's black-and-white and blue all over?

A: A penguin shivering in the cold

Private: I'm a little hoarse this morning.
Skipper: That's funny, you still look like a penguin to me!

Kowalski: The zoo tourists are always taking my picture and asking me to smile.
Skipper: I guess you have to pen-grin and bear it.

Private: Why are we fishing at night?
Skipper: So we can catch *star*fish.

Skipper: What does Rico say after an all-you-can-eat buffet?
Kowalski: *Burp!*

Skipper: What's Rico's favorite drink?
Kowalski: Cough-ee, of course.

Private: Rico has a new gadget but he won't tell anyone what it is.
Skipper: Did you ask him?
Private: I told him to just spit it out.

←Dolphin

Depth

Lemur

SKIPPER'S TOP TEN REASONS FOR HIRING THE PENGUINS OF MADAGASCAR FOR YOUR COMMANDO OPERATION

1. We lay everything out in black-and-white.

2. If something smells fishy, we take care of it. Or we eat it.

3. No matter what the task, we dive right in.

4. When plans go wrong, we can just wing it.

5. We know how to put a freeze on crime.

6. We have twenty-four–hour Web access— on our feet.

7. Our team can stomach any cold weather.

8. We can go undercover underwater.

9. When the mission is accomplished, we are already dressed in tuxedos for the afterparty.

10. You want tough? We're penguins that live in New York City! It doesn't get much tougher than that.

Q: WHY DID THE PENGUIN CROSS THE ICE ON HIS STOMACH?

A: TO GET TO THE OTHER SLIDE

Q: WHAT'S A PENGUIN'S FAVORITE PART OF A DONUT?

A: *THE FROSTING*

Q: WHY DO PENGUINS MAKE GREAT PANCAKES?

A: *BECAUSE THEY HAVE THEIR OWN FLIPPERS*

Kowalski: I'm getting ready for my favorite winter sport.
Private: Sledding?
Kowalski: Kowalskiing!

Skipper: We've been asked to rescue a stranded surgeon.
Private: What are we going to call the mission?
Skipper: Operation Operation.

Skipper: Knock, knock.
Private: Who's there?
Skipper: Waddle.
Private: Waddle who?
Skipper: Waddle I do till you answer the door?

Private: A penguin just sailed a boat around the world.
Skipper: I don't believe it.
Private: Why not?
Skipper: It sounds like a *ferry* tale to me.

King Julien: I did not know penguins could fly.

Mort: They can't.

King Julien: Tell that to Skipper. He just got on a rocket ship.

Private: I'm making our favorite meal.

Kowalski: Tuna smoothies?

Private: No, *chilly* con carne.

Q: WHAT DO YOU CALL A PENGUIN RAPPER?

A: *SNOOP BIRDD*

Q: WHAT DO YOU CALL A PENGUIN WITH TOO CLOSE A SHAVE?

A: *NICK*

Q: WHAT DO YOU CALL A PENGUIN WHO LIKES TO DRUM?

A: *TOM-TOM*

Lemur Laughs

Q: WHAT DO YOU CALL LOUD LEMURS?

A: SCREAMER LEMURS

Q: WHAT DO YOU CALL LEMURS WITH THEIR HEADS IN THE CLOUDS?

A: DREAMER LEMURS

Q: WHAT DO YOU CALL SNEAKY LEMURS?

A: SCHEMER LEMURS

Q: WHAT KIND OF CARS DO LEMURS DRIVE?

A: LEMUR BEAMERS

Skipper: I heard King Julien got a new automobile.

Private: Really? What kind?

Skipper: A Madagas-*car*.

Marlene: Last night while King Julien was asleep, Mort snuck in and tickled his feet.

Phil: He must have been upset.

Marlene: He told me he was *Mort*-ified.

Q: What do you call King Julien when he sits on top of the tallest tree in the jungle?

A: *Your high-ness*

Q: If Shakespeare were a lemur, what play would he write?

A: *Romeo and Julien*

RULES OF THE ROYAL COURT

1. A private audience with King Julien must be requested a month in advance. Unless you have gifts. Then come on in!
2. Don't even think about touching the feet.
3. Do not look King Julien in the eyes. Instead, focus your attention on his magnificent ringtail.
4. You may address King Julien one of three ways. Your Highness, Your Highness, and finally, Your Highness.

Maurice: Hey, what's that noise?
King Julien: It's my new ringtail tone.

Kowalski: What did King Julien say to the gecko around his head?
Skipper: Quit crowning around.

King Julien: I want to have a royal party and invite everyone.
Maurice: Including Marlene?
King Julien: Let's Skipper.
Maurice: What about Phil and Mason?
King Julien: It's Private.
Maurice: Bada and Bing, the gorillas?
King Julien: They'll just Ric-o havoc.
Maurice: The hippos?
King Julien: Of course they can come.
Maurice: Why them and no one else?
King Julien: Because I cannot think of a pun for Kowalski.

Q: What do you call an early rising lemur?

A: *Dawn*

Q: What do you call a lawyer lemur?

A: *Sue*

Q: What do you call a moving lemur?

A: *Van*

Maurice: Knock, knock.
Mort: Who's there?
Maurice: Justin.
Mort: Justin who?
Maurice: Justin time to answer the door!

King Julien: Did I ever show you the battle mark on my tail from defending the Lemur Kingdom?
Maurice: No, Your Highness.
King Julien: I call it my Madaga-scar.

ANIMAL CRACK-UPS!

Q: WHERE DO PENGUINS PLAY ON THE PLAYGROUND?

A: ON THE BLACK-AND-WHITE TOP

Q: WHERE DO LEMURS PLAY ON THE PLAYGROUND?

A: THE JUNGLE GYM

Q: WHERE DO MASON AND PHIL PLAY ON THE PLAYGROUND?

A: ON THE MONKEY BARS

Q: WHERE DO TIGERS PLAY ON THE PLAYGROUND?

A: ANYWHERE THEY WANT TO

Marlene: I can never make a decision.
Private: Why not?
Marlene: It's hard for me to choose between one thing and an otter.

Marlene: I just made the same mistake twice.
Maurice: Why are you so upset?
Marlene: I otter know better.

Maurice: I'm off to see Marlene.
She needs some help.
Mort: You're a good friend.
Maurice: Well, I always told her
she could Mar*lene* on me.

Marlene: The new monkey dad has
a bad attitude.
Maurice: How so?
Marlene: Seems he has a small chimp
on his shoulder.

Phil: Knock, knock.
Mason: Who's there?
Phil: Banana.
Mason: Banana who?
Phil: Knock, knock.
Mason: Who's there?
Phil: Banana.
Mason: Banana who?
Phil: Knock, knock.
Mason: Who's there?
Phil: Orange.
Mason: Orange who?
Phil: Orange you happy I finally stopped saying banana?

Skipper: Phil and Mason have started a new shoe polishing business.
Kowalski: That's great. What do they call it?
Skipper: Monkeyshines.

Private: Why do Phil and Mason love bananas?
Skipper: Because they are so a-peeling.

Phil: I need to send flowers to a sick friend.
Mason: What kind are you going to pick?
Phil: Chimp-pansys.

Phil: My fur is really dry.
Mason: You have to use more chimp-poo and conditioner.

Phil: Knock, knock.
Mason: Who's there?
Phil: Monkey see monkeed.
Mason: Monkey see monkeed who?
Phil: That's right! Monkey see, monkey do!

Mason: One of my cousins is an astronaut on a one-year mission.
Phil: You must miss him a lot.
Mason: Not really. I get daily updates on Spacebook.

Phil: Why are the other chimps so lazy?
Mason: Because all they do is hang around all day.

Mason: They discovered my grandfather was a genius.
Phil: That's why you're so smart.
Mason: I guess you could say I'm a chimp off the old block.

NeW ANiMaL IteMS ON SaLe at tHe ZOOVENir SHOP!

- King Julien Doll with Battery-Powered Moneymaker, $6.99
- *Mason and Phil's Guide to Sign Language,* $2.99
- Marlene's "I Heart Squirrels" Bumper Sticker, $1.99
- Mort's Royal Foot Cream— it brings out the king in you!, $10.99
- *The Penguins of Madagascar Cookbook* featuring Skipper's Fresh Fish Smoothies and Marlene's Pasta with Popcorn Sauce, $15.00

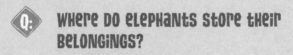

Q: Where do elephants store their belongings?

A: *In their trunks*

Q: What do elephants do when it rains?

A: *They take out their umbrella-phants.*

Skipper: What's Phil and Mason's favorite dessert?
Kowalski: Chocolate *chimp* cookies.

Skipper: How do you say good-bye to Roger?
Kowalski: See you later, alligator.

Q: Did you hear about the ape date?
A: *It was typical boy meets gorilla.*

Q: Did you hear the one about the seal that went crazy?
A: *He totally flippered out.*

Q: Did you hear the one about the glad hippo?
A: *He was a happy-potamus.*

Q: Did you hear the one about the rapper hippo?
A: *He was a hip-hop-apotamus.*

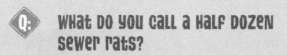

Q: WHAT DO YOU CALL A HALF DOZEN SEWER RATS?

A: A SIX-PACK

Q: Why do hornets make such a loud buzz?
A: *They're having a sting-along.*

Private: Sir, I think I just made the nest of hornets very angry.
Skipper: What did you do?
Private: I told them to buzz off.

King Julien: I'm naming Bada and Bing as the official BBQ chefs to the Royal Court.
Maurice: Why?
King Julien: Because all the food is fresh off the gorill-a.

Private: I invited Joey the kangaroo to join us for dinner, but he just wants to stay home and watch TV.

Skipper: I guess he's a real *pouch* potato.

Q: WHAT DO YOU CALL A KANGAROO IN A BAD MOOD?

A: KANGA-RUDE

Q: WHAT'S A KANGAROO'S FAVORITE MUSIC?

A: HIP-HOP, OF COURSE!

Q: HOW DOES A KANGAROO DELIVER A LETTER?

A: IN ITS MAIL POUCH

Q: How do you tease a poisonous frog?
A: *Rib it, rib it, rib it*

Skipper: Why is Dr. Blowhole the dolphin a saltwater animal?
Kowalski: Why?
Skipper: Because no one wants to swim in pepper water.

Julien: What do you say to Dr. Blowhole when his blowhole spouts water?
Mort: I don't know, what?
Julien: Say it, don't spray it.

Marlene: The raccoon just stole the tires off Alice's cart.
Maurice: I guess he is the rubber-bandit.

Q: Why is a chameleon like a kitchen mixer?
A: *Because they both blend in.*

Q: Why is every day Halloween for raccoons?
A: *Because they never take off their masks.*

Q: WHAT DO YOU CALL A SNAKE WITH A TINY PIECE OF WOOD IN IT?

A: *A SLITHER SLIVER*

Q: HOW DO YOU WEIGH A SNAKE?

A: *BY ITS SCALES, OF COURSE*

Q: WHAT LANGUAGE DO FALCONS SPEAK?

A: *WINGSPAN-ISH*

New York Zoo Funnies!

Private: Hey, did you here about the new pig exhibit at the zoo?
Kowalski: No.
Private: They're calling it "New Pork zoo."

Private: Did you hear about the new oxen exhibit at the zoo?
Kowalksi: No.
Private: They're calling it "New Yak zoo."

King Julien: I heard Alice was very upset about the wild zoo party last night.
Maurice: What happened?
King Julien: She said everyone was behaving like animals.

Skipper: Alice wants to put artificial snow in our penguin lair.
Private: I wonder what it's made of.
Skipper: Snow-fakes.

Private: I'm creating a new recipe for the park picnic.
Skipper: What's in it?
Private: Snow peas and iceberg lettuce.
Skipper: Then you should call it cold-slaw.

Private: If I may say so, sir, your singing for the zoo talent show sounds off-key.
Skipper: Thanks for the feedback. I must be out of *tuna*.

Private: The zoo popcorn is the most wonderful, incredible, delicious popcorn I've ever had.
Skipper: It's just a bucket of popcorn. Why all the praise?
Private: Because you have to keep buttering it up.

Marlene: Would you like to come over for dinner?
Private: Sure, what are we having?
Marlene: *Marlene* cuisine.

Private: The zoo doctor is out of town, so the ducks referred me to theirs.
Kowalski: Aren't you afraid he'll be a *quack*?
Private: That's okay, they said he'll *bill* me later.

SKIPPER'S RULES FOR THE ZOO

1. Do not feed the animals. Except for the penguins.
2. Try not to point at the monkeys and imitate them. They might throw poo at you.
3. Alice is the zookeeper. Feel free to throw popcorn at her and ask her silly questions.
4. Do not take flash photos of the elephants. They don't like it. Their trunks are full of water, and they're not afraid to use them.
5. Stay with the buddy your teacher assigns you at all times. Unless your buddy falls into the alligator pond.
6. You are not actually observing us. We are observing you. And you are very entertaining.
7. There are souvenirs for sale after the tour. The plush penguins are especially cute.
8. Did I mention feeding the penguins?

Private: I don't like the new plush toy of me in the Zoovenir Shop.
Skipper: How come?
Private: It shows me eating a whole bucket of fish!
Skipper: Why is that a problem?
Private: I'm already stuffed.

Skipper: Boys, there's a new snow globe of us in the Zoovenir Shop.
Private: I don't want to see it.
Skipper: Why not?
Private: It gives me the shakes.

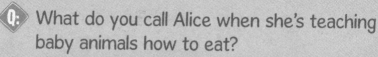

Q: What do you call Alice when she's teaching baby animals how to eat?
A: *A chew-chew trainer*

Q: What do you call Alice when she's jumping?
A: *A leaper zookeeper*

Q: What do you call Alice when she's napping?
A: *A sleeper zookeeper*

Skipper: I was thinking of getting a drawing of our bunker inked on my flipper.
Kowalski: That's nice.
Skipper: It'll be my habitat-too.

Skipper: It was too hot in the bunker last night.
Kowalski: I'll adjust the *lair* conditioning.

Private: I was watching the pigeons in the park eat stale bread, and I felt kind of bad.
Skipper: Why?
Skipper: Because their diet is so *crumby*.

Q: WHY IS IT DIFFICULT TO ESCAPE FROM THE ZOO?

A: IT'S A VERY HARD HABITAT TO BREAK.

Q: WHAT'S THE BEST-SELLING TOY AT THE ZOOVENIR SHOP?

A: THE KAZOO

Skipper: All right, men, last night we had water leaking in our bunks.
Private: What happened?
Skipper: The zoo-er backed up.

Skipper: There was a crazy pigeon in our bunker last night.
Private: How could you tell?
Skipper: He kept saying, "Coo-coo, coo-coo!"

Private: I didn't know they were running a marathon through the zoo today.
Skipper: That's no marathon—the tiger escaped!

Marlene: Did you hear about the school kid who fell in the New York zoo?
Maurice: No.
Marlene: It was a real field *trip*.